This book belongs to

_____

_____

Lonely Wasp

To Megan

Lonely
Wasp

Charles Fuge & Vicki Churchill

OXFORD
UNIVERSITY PRESS

Nobody wanted to be friendly with Wasp.
All the other creatures were frightened of
him, as soon as they saw his stripey
colours and heard him buzz.

A ladybird was snoozing nearby.
'Good morning,' said Wasp, in a friendly way.

But the ladybird flew away.

An interesting-looking fellow was making
his way along a mossy branch.
'Good morning,' said Wasp politely.

Woodlouse gave a look of terror and dropped off the branch.

And as for Snail . . .

Wasp edged carefully over to the
dandelion patch.
'Good m–'
But Snail was already off, with only
a backward glance.

'No one will be my friend.' Wasp was
very sad. Buzzing miserably, he spun
round and sped . . .

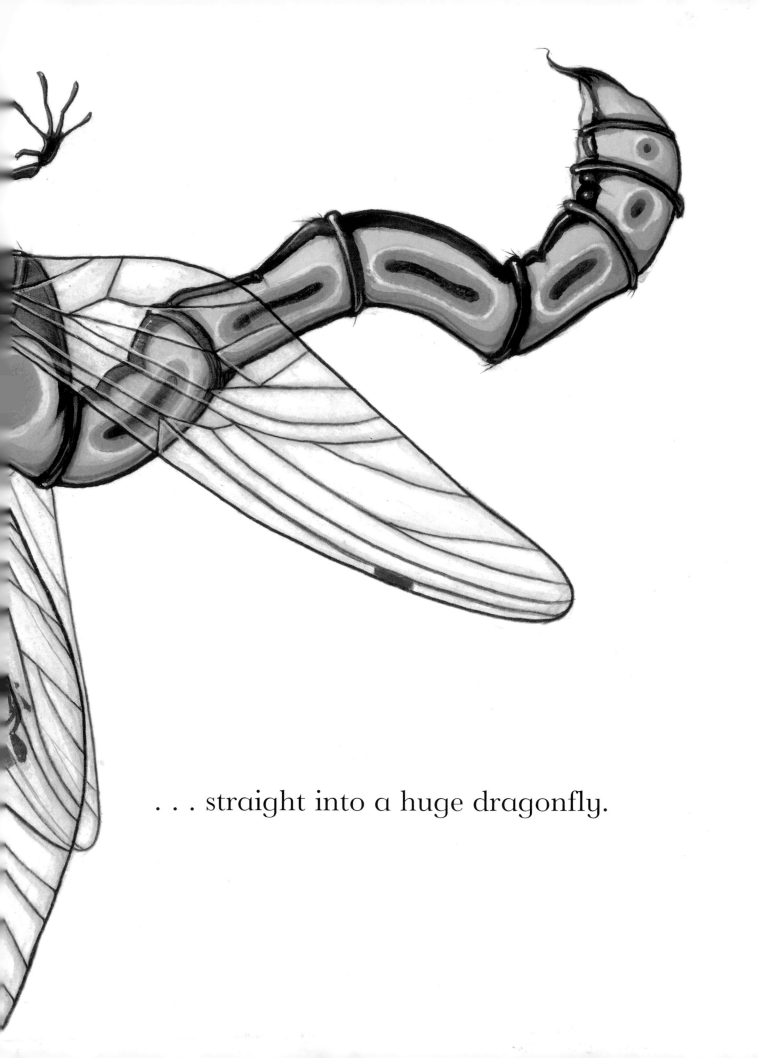

. . . straight into a huge dragonfly.

'Look where you're going, little one,' said the dragonfly, in a friendly way. He wasn't afraid of anybody. The sound of a kind voice was too much for Wasp. He started to sniffle – and the whole story came out.

'Don't worry,' said Dragonfly,
'I'll take you under my wing.
Come with me.'
And together they flew off.

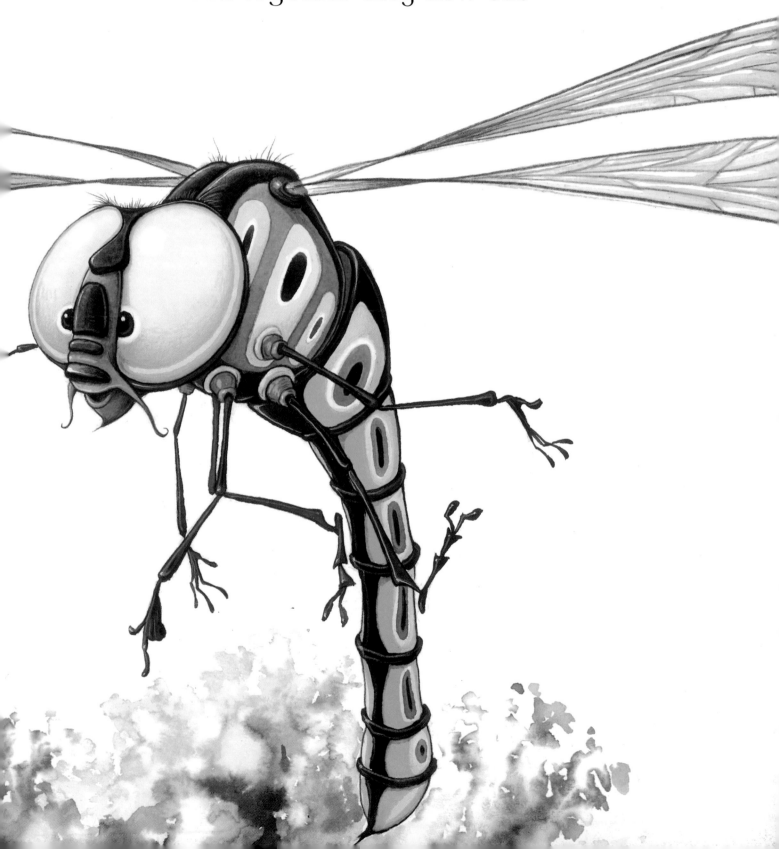

'Meet *my* friends,' called
Dragonfly, proudly.
Wasp was confused.
He couldn't see anybody,
just leaves and twigs.
Was it all a trick
to tease him?

Then the leaf stood up!
'Hello,' he said.
It was Cricket.

'Cricket pretends to be a
leaf so that he can hide,'
explained Dragonfly.

Then the twig stood
up and bowed.

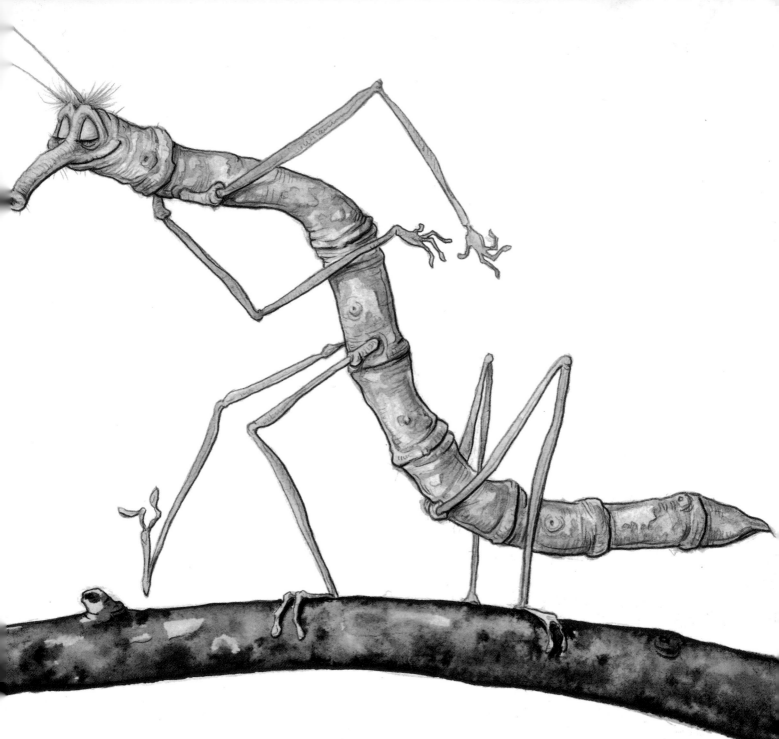

'Meet my friend Stick Insect,' said
Cricket. 'He hides by pretending to be
a twig.'
'That's really clever,' said Wasp.
'But hides from what?'

'From ME!' roared a voice. 'And
I'm looking for my BREAKFAST!'
Cricket and Stick Insect froze. Dragonfly
sped away. But the little wasp didn't hesitate . . .

Buzzing angrily, he dived
straight at the blubbery
beast as it licked its fat
warty lips.

In and out he darted,
dodging Toad's sticky
lightning tongue.
The toad lunged back.

Then Wasp did what wasps do best. He gave Toad a nasty sting. That was enough for Toad. Tired and sore, he crept back under his stone.

Wasp's new friends clapped and cheered.
'Hooray for Wasp! Wasp has saved us all!
No other insect was brave enough to see off Toad.'

The happiest of all was Wasp. His search was over, for now he had three special friends.

OXFORD
UNIVERSITY PRESS

Great Clarendon Street, Oxford OX2 6DP

Oxford University Press is a department of the University of Oxford.
It furthers the University's objective of excellence in research, scholarship,
and education by publishing worldwide in

Oxford New York

Athens Auckland Bangkok Bogotá Buenos Aires Calcutta
Cape Town Chennai Dar es Salaam Delhi Florence Hong Kong Istanbul
Karachi Kuala Lumpur Madrid Melbourne Mexico City Mumbai
Nairobi Paris São Paulo Singapore Taipei Tokyo Toronto Warsaw

with associated companies in Berlin Ibadan

Oxford is a registered trade mark of Oxford University Press
in the UK and in certain other countries

British Library Cataloguing in Publication Data available

ISBN 0 19 279040 4 Hardback
ISBN 0 19 272379 0 Paperback

1 3 5 7 9 10 8 6 4 2

Typeset by Oxford Designers & Illustrators, Oxford

Printed in Hong Kong

Other OXFORD books you may enjoy

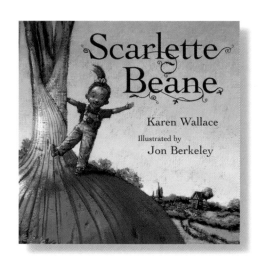

Scarlette Beane

Karen Wallace

Illustrated by
Jon Berkeley

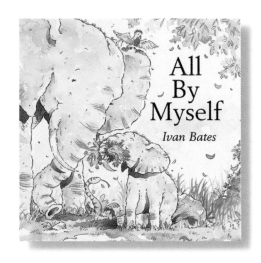

All By Myself

Ivan Bates

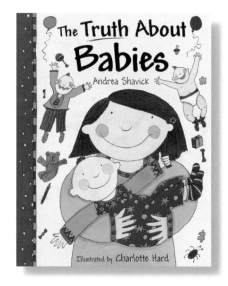

The Truth About Babies

Andrea Shavick

Illustrated by Charlotte Hard

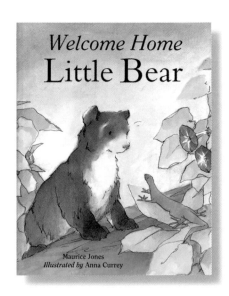

Welcome Home Little Bear

Maurice Jones
Illustrated by Anna Currey